# HALLOWEEN PARTY

For Geneva Peterson—
my Aunt Bee, who was born on Halloween

First Edition    2    3    4    5    6    7    8    9    10

Library of Congress Cataloging in Publication Data
Shute, Linda. Halloween party / by Linda Shute.
p.    cm.    Summary: Costumes, monsters, and food abound at the tempting, teasing, terrible Halloween
party that happens once each year.    ISBN 0-688-11714-7.—ISBN 0-688-11715-5 (lib. bdg.)    [1. Halloween—Fiction.
2. Parties—Fiction.    3. Stories in rhyme.]    I. Title.    PZ8.3.S5599Hal    1994    [E]—dc20    93-25215    CIP    AC

# HALLOWEEN PARTY

BY LINDA SHUTE

LOTHROP, LEE & SHEPARD BOOKS    NEW YORK

Take my hand and hold it tight!
We'll join the Goblin Band tonight
To dance and play by the full moon's light
At the spooky, scary, once-a-year Halloween Party

We put on our costumes and fasten our masks—
Just say I'm Dracula if anyone asks.
We'll keep our secret as long as it lasts
At the faking, fooling, bamboozling Halloween party.

Down dark and foggy streets we go,
Past jack-o-lantern eyes that glow,
Through pools of mist that swirl and flow,
To the daunting, haunting, hair-raising Halloween party.

On this night when witches prowl,
We jump at the hoot of old Mr. Owl,
And squeak through the gate as black cats yowl,
To the ghostly, ghastly, goose-bumpy Halloween party.

The decorations are all sublime:
Buckets of worms, bowls of slime,
Cobwebby corners where spiders climb
At the dusty, musty, marvelous Halloween party.

Mysterious monsters will greet us there,
Wizards and wombats from who-knows-where,
Medusa with snakes instead of hair
At the freaky, friendly, fabulous Halloween party.

There are devil's food cupcakes and games for all.
While I bob for apples, Gypsy Jane reads her ball.
"Pin the tail on the wolf, you ape, not the wall!"
It's a yelling, yacking, wisecracking Halloween party.

Near midnight, we open the music chest
And pick out the instruments we like the best.
I take the bagpipes and leave them the rest
For a thrumming, drumming, string-strumming Halloween party.

Our tuning up sounds gruesomely sweet.
We sway to the time, then pick up the beat,
Piping faster and louder till ghouls tap their feet
At the snazzy jazzy jamboree Halloween party

We stomp and spin and play a blue streak,
Building our din to a deafening peak.
At the top of the uproar, we all stop and shriek:

Lights on!

Masks off!

**Surprise!**

**Surprise!**

We call out our thank-yous
and say our good-byes,

Then hurry home faster than Mr. Owl flies
From the weird and wonderful, once-a-year Halloween party.